This book belongs to
my friend:

PEXTONR

A NOTE TO PARENTS

Establishing a bedtime routine is a universal experience for most families with young children. For preschoolers, these nightly rounds often feature a favorite blanket or stuffed toy. In *Where Is Polka Dots?*, Blue completes her bedtime ritual only to find that she has misplaced her favorite toy. She uses some clever sleuthing and problem solving to answer the mystery.

As you read the story, encourage your child to compare Blue's bedtime routine to what happens in your house. What is similar? What is different? When Blue realizes that Polka Dots is missing, ask your child to suggest ways Blue can find Polka Dots. As Blue retraces her steps, foster your child's critical-thinking skills by asking him to predict where Blue will go next. Be sure to point out visual as well as textual clues.

As a fun extension to this story, make a bedtime poster with your child. Draw pictures or take photographs of each task that is part of your child's bedtime routine. Talk about which step comes first, second, and so on. Putting a colorful sticker on the poster each night after all the steps are completed could turn what can be a struggle into an enjoyable routine!

Learning Fundamental: 🧩 **problem solving**

For more parent and kid-friendly activities, go to www.nickjr.com.

Where Is Polka Dots?

Published by Scholastic Inc., 90 Old Sherman Turnpike, Danbury, CT 06816

SCHOLASTIC and associated logos are trademarks and/or registered trademarks of Scholastic Inc.

ISBN 0-7172-6621-4

Printed in the U.S.A.

First Scholastic Printing, October 2002

Where Is Polka Dots?

by
Samantha Berger

illustrated by
David Levy

SCHOLASTIC INC.

New York   Toronto   London   Auckland   Sydney
Mexico City   New Delhi   Hong Kong   Buenos Aires

It was the end of a very busy day
for Blue and her friends. They had painted pictures,
played in the sandtable, and put on a puppet
show. Now Blue was getting sleepy.

"I think it's time to start getting ready for bed,"
Blue told her friends. "See you tomorrow," she
said, waving good-bye.

Blue still had lots of things to do before bed. First, she went into the kitchen.

"*Allo*, Blue!" said Mr. Salt. "Would you like to have a bedtime snack with us?"

"Yes, please!" said Blue.

Everyone dipped graham crackers in milk. When
they were finished, Mrs. Pepper said, "Look, the sun
has gone down. It's almost time for bed."

"You're right," said Blue. "Thank you for the snack."

"Good night, Blue!" they all said.

Next, Blue went into the bathroom to take a bath. She and Slippery Soap washed and splashed and made lots of bubbles!

After the bubble bath, Blue brushed her teeth.
Slippery sang a brushing song:
"Brush side to side and up and down.
Brush, brush, brush, brush all around!"

Blue giggled, but it was hard for
her to sing along with toothpaste in her mouth!

After they were finished, Blue yawned. Slippery said,
"You look sleepy, Blue. It's almost time for bed."

Blue stretched and said, "Okay. Good night, Slippery!"

Next, Blue went to the closet to get her pajamas.
She chose her favorite pair and put them on just
right—zipper in front, flap in back! Then it was time
to read a bedtime story.

Blue curled up in the Thinking Chair with her favorite book. Right in the middle of the story, she began to fall asleep.

"I think it really is time for bed now," said Sidetable Drawer.

"Yes," whispered Blue sleepily. "Good night, Sidetable."

Tickety Tock was waiting for Blue in the bedroom.
Blue climbed into bed and snuggled under the covers.
"Good night, Tickety," whispered Blue.
"Good night, Blue," Tickety said softly.

"Good night, Polka Dots," Blue said, as she reached over to give her favorite stuffed animal a hug. Polka Dots slept right next to Blue every single night. But Polka Dots wasn't there. "Wait a minute!" said Blue, sitting up. "Where is Polka Dots?"

"Wake up, Tickety," whispered Blue. "Have you seen Polka Dots?"

"No, not tonight," Tickety said sleepily.

"Where could Polka Dots be?" Blue asked herself.

She thought and thought and thought and thought.
She tried to recall the last time she had seen Polka Dots.
Finally, she had an idea. "I'll try to remember everything
I did before bed to find out where I left Polka Dots."

"Hmm. What was the last thing I did before I went to bed?" Blue tried to remember. "I know! I read a story."

Blue ran to the Thinking Chair. But Polka Dots wasn't there. All she saw was Sidetable Drawer, who was fast asleep.

"I guess Polka Dots wasn't here when I read my book," whispered Blue.

"What did I do before I read my book?" Blue asked herself. "I remember! I put on my pajamas."

Blue ran to the closet. But when she looked inside, Polka Dots wasn't there either.

"I don't think Polka Dots was with me
when I put on my pajamas," Blue sighed.

"Let's see," thought Blue. "What did I do before I put on my pajamas? Oh, I brushed my teeth!"

Blue ran into the bathroom. But when she looked around the sink, there was no Polka Dots. All she saw was Slippery Soap, who was sound asleep and snoring.

"So, when I brushed my teeth, Polka Dots wasn't here," Blue said quietly.

"What did I do before I brushed my teeth?" Blue thought to herself. "I know! I took a bubble bath." Blue tiptoed up to the bathtub and looked all around it. Polka Dots wasn't near the bathtub either.

"Polka Dots isn't in the bathroom," said Blue.

"Where was I before my bath?" Blue wondered.
"I remember! I had a snack."
Blue ran into the kitchen as fast as she could.

"Are you in here, Polka Dots?" she called softly.
Blue peeked over the countertop. "There you are!"
she exclaimed through lots of giggles.

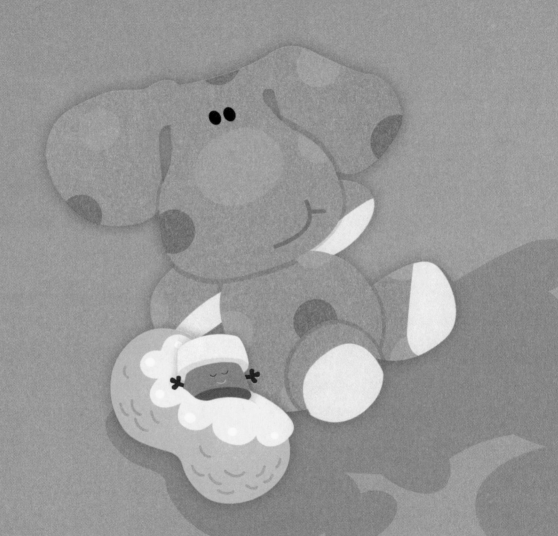

Blue had finally found Polka Dots! She reached
out quietly to take her back to bed. Then she
suddenly stopped.

"Polka Dots and Cinnamon both look very comfortable," she thought. Blue was glad to see her friends look so happy.

Blue tiptoed back to bed. "I know Polka Dots isn't lost, and I know she's helping Cinnamon sleep," Blue said to herself. Pulling the covers up tight, she smiled. "So Polka Dots can sleep with Cinnamon . . .

. . . just for tonight."